W9-BRX-271

TEMPLE ISRAEL LIBRARY
BOSTON. MASS.

NO GOOD IN ART

Story by **Miriam Cohen**
Pictures by **Lillian Hoban**

Greenwillow Books
New York

Text copyright ©1980 by Miriam Cohen
Illustrations copyright ©1980 by Lillian Hoban
All rights reserved. No part of this book
may be reproduced or utilized in any form
or by any means, electronic or mechanical,
including photocopying, recording or by any
information storage and retrieval system,
without permission in writing from the Publisher.

Published by Greenwillow Books
A Division of William Morrow & Company, Inc.
105 Madison Avenue, New York, N.Y. 10016
Printed in the United States of America
First Edition
10 9 8 7 6 5 4 3 2 1

**Library of Congress
Cataloging in Publication Data**

Cohen, Miriam.
No good in art.
Summary: A first-grader is convinced
he can't draw, but when encouraged,
demonstrates he can.
[1. Drawing–Fiction. 2. School stories]
I. Hoban, Lillian. II. Title.
PZ7.C6628No [E] 79-16566
ISBN 0-688-80234-6
ISBN 0-688-84234-8 lib. bdg.

For two wonderful educators-through-art,
Ruth Straus Gainer and Elaine Pear Cohen,
and their book, *Art: Another Language for Learning*

When Jim was in kindergarten, the art teacher said, "Dear, your man has no neck." Then she took Jim's brush and said, "You ought to make your grass with *thin* lines like this."

And she painted her grass
right on his picture.

But in first grade the class got another art teacher.
She asked, "Do you ever think what you want
to be when you get big?"
Everyone nodded.

"How would you like to paint
a picture about it?" she asked.
"Yes! Yes!" everyone shouted.
Then the first grade set to work.

Danny was telling everybody about his picture. "Look! I'm a doctor!"
The doctor was all painted white except for his eyeglasses.
He was reaching inside a lying-down man and pulling things out.
"This is his heart! This is his stomach!" Danny told the kids.

Then he made the doctor pull out two big shoes.
"These are his galoshes!"
Willy and George laughed and laughed.

Margaret was painting a lady dancing. She had a front and a side and a back head. In sparkles on her whirling dress it said MARGARET.

"What a good idea to draw three heads!
That's just the way it looks
when you turn very fast,"
the art teacher said.

After the first grade's trip to the museum,
Willy drew only pictures of whales. This whale
was so big it touched all the edges of the paper.

It had special strainer teeth like whales have.
Willy printed FINBACK WHALE on the bottom.
"I think Willy is going to be a scientist,"
said the art teacher, "he knows so much
about whales."

Sammy made a fire engine driving across the paper.
Speed-puffs were coming out all around,
it was rushing so fast to the fire.

At the end of the hook and ladder was Sammy!

Louie took a crayon and drew little flowers everywhere.
Each flower had a tiny face. Some had kitten faces,
some had grandfather faces with whiskers, some wore eyeglasses,
some had big noses, some were laughing, some were crying.

TEMPLE ISRAEL LIBRARY
BOSTON. MASS.

"Are you in the picture?" asked the art teacher. Louie pointed
to a little face–it was Louie! "What a lovely picture,"
the art teacher said.

Sara was going to be a lawyer because her mother was a lawyer.
George said, "I'm Star-Fighter Man *and* the Dreadable Hunk!"

Anna Maria was a dentist.
There was a little man in her chair.
"Drill! Drill! Drill!"
she was saying.

Only Jim was not painting.
Paul said, "Why don't you
make a picture?"
"I'm no good in art," said Jim.
"Yes, you are," said Paul.

And Anna Maria told Jim,

"Some people are worse than you."

"But my grass is too fat! My men don't have necks!"

Jim hit his head with his hand.

"And I don't even know what I want to be!"

The art teacher heard. She said,
"Why don't you paint a picture
of something you like to *do*?"
Jim shook his head.

But after she had gone to help somebody else,
he moved his brush in a red circle around
the paper. Then he squashed big yellow
blots on the red.

By mixing yellow and blue, he got green, and he made little green lines next to the yellow, and slippery blue all around. Jim kept thinking of more and more ways to make it beautiful.

But the art teacher was saying, "Oh, I'm sorry, it's time
to clean up. Put your name on your picture and give it to me."

Jim hid his picture under the desk and went to clean his brushes.
Willy and Sammy looked at one another.

They grabbed Jim's picture from under the desk and handed it to the art teacher with their own.

When all the pictures
were hanging up,
lots of kids stayed
in front of one.
"It's good!" they said.
"It's pretty!"

"That blue is just like my gramma's dress!"
"I like the green on top of the red."
"The person used good paint."
"It's good to use a lot of paint all around."
"But there's no name! Whose is it?"

Willy and Sammy ran to the sink. They pulled Jim to the front of the room.
"It's Jim's!" they shouted.
"What is it, Jim?" the kids wanted to know.
"It's me, eating pizza," Jim said. "Here's the red pizza, and
the yellow cheese, and some green peppers."

"I wish I had a pizza," George said.

Sara asked, "But what is Jim going to be?"

Willy and Sammy said, "Maybe Jim might be an artist!"

"I think he could be." The art teacher
was smiling at Jim.
"You're good, Jim," said Paul.
Then Jim believed them.
There was the beautiful picture.
And he had made it.